BACK TO CLASS

BACK TO CLASS

poems by
Mel Glenn

photographs by
Michael J. Bernstein

Clarion Books
New York

To Ann, my one and only editor.

M.G.

Acknowledgment

The photographer thanks the teachers and students who agreed to be the models for the photographs in this book.

Clarion Books
a Houghton Mifflin Company imprint
215 Park Avenue South, New York, NY 10003
Text copyright © 1988 by Mel Glenn
Photographs copyright © 1988 by Michael J. Bernstein

Printed in the USA

HAL   10 9 8 7 6 5 4 3 2

Library of Congress Cataloging-in-Publication Data

Glenn, Mel.
  Back to class / poems by Mel Glenn; photographs by Michael J. Bernstein.
      p.   cm.
  Summary: An illustrated collection of sixty-five poems describing a variety of high school students and teachers.
  ISBN 0-89919-656-X
  1. High schools—Poetry.   2. High school students—Poetry.
3. Young adult poetry, American.   [1. High Schools—Poetry.
2. Schools—Poetry.   3. American poetry.]   I. Bernstein, Michael J., ill.   II. Title.
PS3557.L447B33 1988
811'.54—dc19   88-2835
                                   CIP
                                   AC

Author's Note

The characters in this book are fictional composites of the many students and teachers I have worked with through the years. Mr. Robert Winograd, Dennis Finch, Andrea Pulovsky, and all the others live on these pages, not in real life. Yet any resemblance to actual persons is purely intentional in the artistic sense.

Contents

BACK TO CLASS

Mr. Robert Winograd
English
Period 1, Room 102

I met a person at my health club who said,
"You *look* like an English teacher."
How does an English teacher look?
Let me count the ways:
A noun for a nose,
A verb for a vein.
A fragment for a forehead.
Does he conjugate in public
Or only among friends?
Does he speak in complete sentences?
Is his jacket pretty, his face bold?
Wouldn't it be a novel experience
If, just once, I met someone who said,
"Hey, you look like a big-league ballplayer"'?

T. C. Tyler
Period 1, Room 102

Winograd's a real jerk.
Every Friday we write compositions
On another boring topic.
Think he reads them?
No way.
He just returns them a month later
With a little check on the bottom.
Once, in the middle of writing a composition,
This time about my future goals and aspirations,
I indented and wrote down
My mom's recipe for chili,
Did he notice?
Are you kidding?
The little check mark appeared at the bottom.
I could have a cookbook by the end of the term.

Luanne Sheridan
Period 1, Room 102

How can I write a composition
About my future
When I don't even know about my past?
How can I make sense of
What will be
When I don't know what was?
Yeah, they love me.
They're supposed to love me.
They have all the papers, right?
And I love them,
Sort of.
Someday soon, when I finish school,
I'm gonna find my real mother
And make her write
The beginning of this composition.

Dennis Finch
Period 1, Room 102

"My Future—A Personal Essay"

My father has plotted out my future
As if it were a road map:
Starting at point A, he says,
You drive yourself to point B
At the fastest possible speed,
In the shortest possible time.
You keep to the main roads
And never take detours.
I, on the other hand,
Want no part of his plots.
I want to chart my own course,
Throw away his maps
And soar gracefully over the hills
In a big, red, helium-filled balloon,
One that drifts lazily over
The two-lane blacktops of America.
I want to ascend, up to the clouds
That overshadow his points A and B.

Andrea Pulovsky
Period 1, Room 102

Hey man, after first period, I'm history.
Gone.
I'm outta here, real quick.
About one period a day is
All I can stand of this place.
While the teacher is goin' on
About some composition or somethin'
I'm plannin' my own agenda:
    Go out for breakfast,
    Do a bit of shoppin',
    Catch a late-mornin' nap,
    Watch my soaps,
    Maybe invite my boyfriend over
    Before my mother gets home from work.
Hey man, the day's all right,
If you don't let school interfere with it.

Mr. Neil Pressman
Fine Arts
Period 1, Room 105

Last night, I taught you the planets, my son.
You sometimes forgot Mercury,
But once started, you skipped
Through the cosmos with joyful abandon,
Yelling them out in a loud voice of ownership.
If I can't give you the stars
(On a teacher's salary?),
I will give you the planets.
In fact, I will show you how to draw them
And chuckle while you make lopsided circles.
I can tell you, perhaps later, perhaps never,
That I will never be a famous artist myself.
Sssh, that's all right because I can say
In a voice as loud as yours that
I have already created my best piece of art,
One who has sparkled for six delightful years,
One in whose eyes I see a reason
For teaching what I do know and love.

Regina Kelsey
Period 1, Room 105

When it comes right down to it
The only important questions are:
>How far to go,
>How far to let him go,
>How far to let yourself go,
>(Without going too far).
I swear,
It seems less a question of morality
Than of geography.
If I don't, I'm the Last American Virgin.
If I do, I'll get a Reputation.
Naked ladies may be all right for the art world,
But it's more than I can bare.

Gayle Buckingham
Period 1, Room 105

After spending the summer in Paris,
Painting along the Seine,
I told my parents I'd like to see Tahiti next
And follow Gauguin's career.
They told me I have to go to school here
And see how the other half lives.
I have now seen how the other half lives
And much prefer Paris.
Mr. Pressman is all right, I guess,
But part of him seems elsewhere and sad.
In class we're working in pencil.
I use oils, almost exclusively.
I must tell Mr. Pressman
The world is much too colorful
To be penciled in shades of gray.

Herby Wall
Period 1, Room 105

A quick sketch of myself?
Is that what you want, Mr. P.?
I don't know how to do it.
I'm tall,
I'm quiet,
Shy, you might say.
I don't have an outgoing personality.
I don't have a best friend, male or female,
Scared, you might say.
There's nothing special about me
And I can't think of one exceptional thing
    I've done.
I'm the middle child.
My older brother plays football.
My younger sister plays the piano.
Me?
I watch TV and dream a lot.
Here's my drawing—
A stick figure.

Mr. Henry Axhelm
Math
Period 2, Room 107

I teach five classes a day,
Not students, just classes.
No sense getting involved
With their personal problems.
Nothing in their heads worth listening to, anyway.
They came here to socialize,
To see who's "cute."
So I put my x's and y's on the board
And keep my distance.
On Saturdays I like to fool around
With my ham radio set.
It's been my hobby for fifteen years.
I'm on the air for hours at a time.
It's nice to talk to people
Who are far away.

Brent Sorensen
Period 2, Room 107

A modern math problem:
  good grades
+
  good SATs
+
  good interview
+
  good recommendations

= good college.
   Right?
   Not on your life.
   I forgot to
− Subtract the fact
   That everyone else is
   Working with the same figures.

Net
Result: I'm just one more anonymous number
      In the college admissions game.
      It doesn't add up.

Jaime Milagros
Period 2, Room 107

Mr. Axhelm's cool,
Your basic no-frills math teacher.
Here's the problem—
Here's the solution.
In, out, boom, boom, boom!
I wish my life were as simple
As the problems up there on the board.
But how do you figure out
      Who you trust?
      What college to go to?
      Where to find a good job?
      When to get engaged?
      Why my brother uses drugs?
      And, most importantly,
      How to be happy?
I wish Mr. Axhelm could solve
My problems as easily as he solves
The problems up there on the board.

Mallory Wade
Period 2, Room 107

You want me to go to the board
And do that math problem?
You serious?
I'd rather die.
Am I afraid of
      Making a public spectacle of myself,
      Showing the class I'm stupid,
      Tripping over my feet,
      Screeching the chalk along the board,
      Getting the wrong answer or no answer?
You bet!
Get some hotshot like Brent up there.
He eats up this stuff, he's so conceited.
Mr. Axhelm, you know I know the work, sorta.
You know I pass your tests, kinda.
You know I'd do anything you ask, almost.
But please don't make me go up to the board.
I'd rather die.

Kwang Chin Ho
Period 2, Room 141

My family came from China five years ago.
My father holds a doctorate from the university.
He works in a restaurant.
My mother holds an advanced degree from
    the institute.
She works with my father.
The language is easier for me than for them,
Especially Mr. Cantor's language of
Light, magnetism, and motion.
I wish to be an engineer
And build beautiful things.
Every day I go home and
Tell my parents what I have learned.
They nod their heads in approval.
It is then we speak the same language.

Gardner Todd
Period 2, Room 141

Hey, it's gonna be all right.
Yeah, yeah, I'll see you around
. . . maybe.
I've made some plans,
Checked out some arrangements.
Let's just say I've stopped
Worrying about everything, OK?
Hey, it's gonna be all right.
You want my tapes, my ten-speed?
You can have them dirt cheap,
Free in fact.
Yeah, yeah, I'll see you around
. . . maybe.
Hey, it's gonna be all right, I told you.
I'm dead certain about it.

Ms. Emily Parsons
History
Period 3, Room 122

It must have been sixty years ago
When I went up to Sister Ann and asked,
"Should I become a teacher?"
She put her arm around me and said,
"Emily, it's a noble profession, God's work.
Promise me you'll make it your life's calling."
I said yes because I loved her.
I have taught here for nearly forty years.
Some students, some lessons stand out
And even though most years
Have faded into the background
I can still say, even sing out to you,
"Sister Ann, I kept my promise."

Belinda Enriquez
Period 3, Room 122

When I first came to history class
I sat in the last row, last seat
So I could read my romance novels
And not be bothered.
Some teachers notice what I'm reading;
    most don't,
But Miss Parsons did.
She didn't scream,
Or rip the book out of my hands,
Or toss it in the wastebasket.
She just whispered, "Quick, read these,
I've got a million of them—
Real life is better!"
And handed me a list of biographies of
Famous women in history.
I've read many of them—
Harriet Tubman, Joan of Arc, Susan B. Anthony.
I will always remember Miss Parsons's
Gentle smile and right words at the right time.
Maybe I should become a teacher.

Garrett Chandler
Period 3, Room 122

Miss Parsons, surely you jest.
Me fail?
Don't you know who I am?
Let me refresh your memory.
I am
> captain of the quiz team,
> coordinator of the senior show,
> copy editor for the lit magazine.

I am
> president of the debate club,
> point guard for the basketball team,
> peer tutor for the honor society.

I am
> senior section editor for the yearbook,
> student rep for homeroom, and
> salutatorian for this year's class.

Miss Parsons, let's talk this over.
You can't fail me.
I don't have time to study history.
I'm making it instead.

Dawn Weinberg
Period 3, Room 122

The American Revolution,
     War of 1812,
     Civil War,
     Korean War,
     Vietnam War
Can't compare to the
     Skirmishes,
     Clashes,
     Fights,
     Battles,
     Campaigns
That are waged every night at my house
To the dawn's early light.
I put my pillow over my head
To muffle the sound of verbal bullets
That ricochet off the walls.
I wish my parents would call a truce.
But until the day when one side wins
Or the other side breaks off contact
I'll continue to be a prisoner of war.

Ms. Charlotte Kendall
Biology
Period 3, Room 136

After my divorce my world fell apart.
So I threw myself into my work,
Reading the latest literature,
Trying to reach some wandering minds,
Staying up past a reasonable hour
To pump new life into my lesson plans.
I talked to students after school
To show them they were not alone.
I looked for the love in the faces I taught
And thought their polite smiles
Meant more than they did.
One day after helping a student in
    the back of the room,
I returned to my desk to find my purse stolen.
I have to find the love I need elsewhere.

Kristin Leibowitz
Period 3, Room 136

So what's to a relationship?
Most times you're lonely anyway,
But then you meet a guy
And think for a moment that
This one's gonna be different.
Sure.
You date for a few weeks,
Sleep with the guy or
Not sleep with the guy.
Then, instead of seeing him every day,
You're lucky if you see him once a week.
Then, maybe, every other week.
He's working or you're busy.
Is he playin' around?
Soon, you don't see him at all.
Then you meet another guy.
This one's gonna be different.
Sure.

Kyle Quinn
Period 3, Room 136

It's immaterial what I become,
My parents have told me,
As long as I'm
Happy, satisfied
And at peace with myself.
It's very material what I become,
I told them,
I want to be
Successful, wealthy,
And famous in my lifetime.
I told them I want to be a doctor.
"Good," they said. "You'll help the needy."
"Wrong," I said. "I'll have a practice
    in the suburbs."
My parents wonder where they've failed.
They haven't; they've showed me the path.
I just want it carpeted.
Bio may be a bit boring now
(Seriously, will anybody ever ask me
The parts of a paramecium?),
But it's the first step on my road to riches.

Mr. Eugene Worthington
Physical Education
Period 4, Gym

Five minutes before the recent
Student-faculty basketball game
My mind played videotapes of
Fall afternoons when I was fifteen,
When basketball was my consuming passion.
We played for hours before darkness chased us.
Five minutes into the student-faculty game
I realized one can't play from memory.
I dribbled a ball into an opponent's hand
And then threw a pass away.
I blew an easy lay-up
And realized I was playing in the past tense.
My doctor tells me it's an ironic joke,
A gym teacher in such poor shape.
I promised him I will quit smoking
And struggle to regain what is lost
With a sad kind of vigor.

Winston Hines
Period 4, Gym

Measuring my life in points-per-game average,
I felt I was a shoo-in for the
Best player on the team.
When I saw there were other guys better than me
I felt I was a shoo-in for the starting five.
When I saw there were *still* guys better than me
I felt I was a shoo-in for the team.
When I was cut, Mr. Worthington, out of pity,
Appointed me the team manager.
Now I stand on the sidelines,
Basking in the glow of a winning season and
Measuring my life in wet towels and
    Ace bandages.
All my dreams have dribbled away.

Audrey Reynolds
Period 4, Gym

The Beam:

keep my balance

ever   and

I   not

will   go

How   insane?

Deidre Spector
Period 4, Gym

Volleyball:

Shuttled	back
and	forth
between	parents,
I	cannot
tell	where
the	court
will	bounce

me.

Toni Vingelli
Period 4, Gym

The Note:

> Dear Mr. Worthington,
>   I cannot dress for gym for the reasons checked below:
> √ Bubonic plague
> √ My period
> √ Sprained pinkie
> √ Allergic to sweat
> √ Unsafe locker room
> √ Total clod
> √ Just washed hair
> √ Cold floor
> √ Pulled muscle
> Respectfully yours,
>   Toni

"Nice try, Vingelli. Get in line."
"Yessir!"

Ms. Marilyn Lindowsky
Counselor
Period 4, Room 110

You got a problem, kid?
You'll just have to wait on line.
There are too many students ahead of you.
Besides, I probably couldn't help you much anyway,
Not enough time or counselors.
But my paperwork is up-to-date,
Neatly clipped together.
The pregnant, depressed, paranoid, lonely,
All troop through my office,
Casualties of the teenage wars.
Sometimes between the shuffled papers
And stapled forms,
Back-to-class passes
And choked sobs,
I say something that helps for the moment,
An emotional Band-Aid for wounds too large
        to heal.
I hear they're cutting support services again
        next year,
Not enough money even for office supplies.
It's just as well.
I can't hold lives together with paper clips.

Victor Jeffreys
Period 4, Room 110

"Ms. L., I'm in love, but I can't tell anyone."

"Not anyone? You told me."

"That's different, but there are complications."

"A case of different backgrounds?"

"Nope, same background."

"Different religion?"

"Nope, same religion."

"Don't tell me, different race?"

"It should be that easy."

"I've run out of differences, Victor."

"Try same gender."

"Oh. That presents a whole different situation."

"I know."

"What do you want me to say?"

"I don't know, something different,
Something helpful."

Annette Harrison
Period 4, Room 110

It's like this, Ms. L.,
He wants to—definitely.
I want to—maybe.
However,
He wants to be spontaneous and passionate.
I want to be careful and cautious—this time.
He's talking the sun and the moon.
I'm talking relationship and commitment
      —this time.
He's promising to sweep me off my feet.
I'm promising myself to keep vertical
      —this time.
He says we'll have a beautiful future together.
I say let's talk about the present.
He whispers, "Don't you trust me?"
I whisper back, "I don't trust any guy
      —completely."
He says, "You've hurt my feelings."
I say, "I don't care. I'm trusting my own—"
This time.

Jimmy Zale
Period 4, Room 110

You're the one who called me down here, Mrs. L.
I don't have no problem, everything's cool.
Yeah, I know my grades are down, what of it?
And the twenty-nine cuts, no big thing.
My stepfather called?
What did the moron want?
Who asked him to butt in?
My mom and me were doin' OK
Before she married him.
He's always hasslin' me about school,
My friends, my music, everything.
Hey, I don't wanna talk about him, OK?
Yeah, yeah, I'll do better
And I won't cut out, ya happy?
So I lit a couple of matches in class.
You gonna make a big deal about that or what?

Ms. Nadine Sierra
French
Period 5, Room 206

"Barbie."
"Present."
"Betsy."
"Present."
"Raggedy Ann."
"Present."
When I was five I would play "school,"
Lining up the porch chairs,
Telling my dollies how to sit.
When I was fifteen I would study my teachers,
Copying the way they spoke,
Watching the methods they used.
Now that I am twenty-five
And have a classroom of my own,
The past has become my present and
Each day is wonderful, even thrilling.
All my dollies have come to life.
I will teach them, take care of them.
"Nadine."
"Present."

Martine Provencal
Period 5, Room 206

My grandmother sold flowers in the marketplace.
She'd sit under a big hat and sing to me,
Ignoring the searing heat of the island sun.
She'd sing magical, happy songs of
Animals that talked and
Wishes that came true.
Sometimes people would buy flowers,
Most times not.
But they all returned her wide, warm smile.
"I will sell flowers, too," I told her.
"You, child, will bloom in another soil,"
    she said.
When we had to leave our island,
Grandmother stayed behind.
"My roots cannot be moved, little one," she said.
    "Go and be happy."
I find myself humming one of her songs now
As I stare out of the classroom window
And see scraggly trees push through
    cracked concrete.
My grandmother sold flowers in the marketplace.

Jonathan Sobel
Period 5, Room 206

My grandfather told stories in three languages.
When I was a little boy, six or so,
I'd climb into his lap and listen
As he narrated in English, Hebrew, and Yiddish.
If I didn't understand all the words,
I certainly understood the melody of his voice.
I'd notice the numbers branded on his arm
And would playfully add them up,
  forty-three, I remember.
When I asked him about them he said,
"Sssh, *tateleh*, after the stories."
The stories never stopped; he never told me.
Last month, a quick robbery, a sudden bullet
Ended a life that had cheated death
Many years before I was even born.
I find myself thinking of his stories now
As I stare out of the classroom window and
See in my mind's eyes the numbers branded
  on his arm.
They still add up to forty-three.
My grandfather told stories in three languages.

Patricia Lampert
Period 5, Room 206

Whenever a teacher announces a test
I break out into a cold sweat.
A pop quiz is cause for an anxiety attack.
A test is reason enough for a sneezing fit
And a midterm is good for
    massive stomach spasms.
The announcement of a final
Can lay me up for days.
A term paper?
Well, forget it—I break out in hives.
Last week Ms. Sierra said we would have
This humongous test on verbs today.
Armed with Kleenex and yellow legal pads,
I sneezed and studied for three days
Only to find out she had postponed the exam.
I hope real life is never like this.
I couldn't stand the strain.

Mr. Desmond Klinger
Music
Period 5, Room 223

I teach music, hardly noteworthy,
To five groups of heathens a day.
I have been in this school for ten years,
Ten years too long.
I did not trust my own talents or instincts
And now it is too damn late.
I am trapped by my own incompetence.
My son totters on uncertain feet,
Reaching for the piano keys in the living room.
His cereal-faced grin radiates joy
At a future full of jack-in-the-box surprises.
I look at him with envy
And wish for a return to his possibilities.

Valerie O'Neill
Period 5, Room 223

My mother won't let me go out with Nick.
She considers him a sleaze-ball in training,
One step above a convicted felon.
She won't let me
Talk to him on the phone,
See him on the weekends,
Invite him over to the house.
She has threatened to throw me out
If I so much as breathe his name.
Nick and I meet in the halls between class,
Quick kisses made quicker
By bells that know no romance
And clock hands that move too fast.
Sometimes when Mr. Klinger's back is turned,
I sneak out of the room and find Nick.
We slip into a stairwell
And make up for lost time.
The only ringing bells are in my head
And our hands move real slow.

Claud St. Jules
Period 5, Room 223

So I was listening to my Walkman
(It's a music class, right?)
When Mr. Klinger ripped the headphones
Off my ears and put them to his own.
"You call this music?" he said,
Looking at me like I had just landed
    on the planet.
"I've heard better music in drainpipes.
Here is a quarter, go telephone your parents
And tell them you have no musical taste
    whatsoever."
The class thought that was funny.
I didn't—he totally embarrassed me.
Klinger sure wins the prize.
In fact, I'd like to give him one:
For least distinguished performance
By a teacher in a continuous series.
I'd like to tune him out permanently.

Jackie Grant
Period 5, Room 223

Everyone dumps on Klinger.
He's nasty, abusive, sarcastic, and cold—
And that's on one of his good days.
He's the roughest teacher I've ever had.
One time, after school, after
    cheerleading practice,
I heard lovely music coming from his room.
"Beautiful," I said, walking in and sitting down.
"Beethoven," he said, nodding slowly
    and playing on.
Those were the only words spoken.
In the twenty minutes I listened
They were the only words needed.
As I watched his hands dance over the keys
I wondered, how can a man who
Plays so movingly act so mean?
I don't get it.

Ms. Yvonne Harmon
Librarian
Period 6, Library

My parents, putting me through school, said,
"Become a teacher, you'll have summers off.
Better yet, become a librarian.
You've always had your nose in a book anyway."
I believed them because they were my parents.
My parents were proud of me.
I hated them because
I didn't have the courage to say
I didn't want to live their dreams.
                    Now, years later,
My life has turned institutional green
As I check out books without comment.
Perhaps there is still time
To renew my own connection to life.
My parents?
They died last year.
What good is my anger now?

Kumar Ragnath
Period 6, Library

Here in this library
Ms. Harmon has sat with me
And together we looked over the bulletins
For university in this country.
I was unworthy of her time.
She helped me fill out the applications,
Sent away for the financial papers
And told me for which scholarships to apply.
I was unworthy of her effort.
She told me which courses to take,
What program to major in,
What possibilities were in my field.
I was unworthy of her knowledge.
Yesterday I received the joyous news.
I was accepted into technical college.
I am truly worthy now.
May Ms. Harmon be rewarded everlasting.

Janet DeStasio
Period 6, Library

Emily Brontë—how did you do it?
I sit here in the library
Surrounded by thousands of authors
And wonder, how did you dream of a world
Of moors, old mansions, and windswept nights,
Of relationships so complex I have trouble
Keeping my Earnshaws and Lintons apart?
Did you read your first drafts to your sisters?
Did you study best-seller lists of 1845?
Did you rewrite?
I want to know all of this because
I, too, want to be a writer and
Make up characters who are larger than life,
Larger than my own life,
Which is kinda boring.
Emily Brontë—how did you do it?

Andy Fierstein
Period 6, Library

In this library
I've been to London and Tara
And the Great Sahara,
Palm trees in Bali,
Oases in Mali,
Ruins in Greece,
Beaches at Nice,
Yellowstone Park,
Rome after dark,
Cities of China,
North Carolina,
Capital of Bern,
Or maybe Lucerne,
Fiords of Norway,
Within this doorway,
Someday,
Bombay,
Or maybe the Nile,
Depends what's in the catalogue file.

Mr. John Fletcher
Chemistry
Period 6, Room 236

I wanted to be a doctor,
But I didn't get into med school.
I wanted to be a research scientist,
But I couldn't finish my PhD.
I could say it was
Lack of money or lack of ambition,
But the truth is I wasn't smart enough.
Here in high school you stay
One chapter ahead of the kids.
Teaching is a wonderful profession
For those whose dreams have died elsewhere.
Save your sympathy, though,
I'm doing what I can
With what I've got.

Nicholas Townshed
Period 6, Room 236

The bomb dropped a year ago
When my parents told me
They were getting a divorce.
As an eerie calm hovered around ground zero,
    the kitchen table,
I watched the night sky explode
In flashing arguments and blinding accusations,
I watched the destruction of my nuclear family.
The theater of our conflict has since cooled
As I have made some small peace
With my father's new girlfriend
And my mother's new boyfriend.
I still feel the fallout of sadness
Which hangs over my house
Like a dark, reddish cloud.
The fallout from the divorce
Still leaves me sick to my stomach.
I continue to suffer from the aftershocks.

Arnold Flitterman
Period 6, Room 236

Bad chemistry exists between me and Mr. Fletcher,
Ever since the time he mixed two liquids together
And asked, "Flitterman, what do we have here?"
Not knowing the right answer,
But seeing a green slime ooze from the beaker
I said, "A mess, sir."
He was not amused and gave me a zero.
"But that's *my* reaction," I said, protesting.
He gave me another zero.
"Can you express chemically
The equation that happened here?" he persisted.
"No," I said.
"It's in the text," he added.
"I didn't read it," I responded.
"Another zero," he said, triumphantly.
I didn't care,
It's usually so boring in this class that
Sometimes you just gotta come up with
Your own formula for having fun.

Ms. Phyllis Shaw
Speech
Period 7, Room 202

Come in, seventh-period class.
Welcome to the festivities.
It is nearly the end of the day
As well as the end of my patience.
You have made your position quite clear
Issuing your White Paper on Indifference.
But, my darlings, I don't give up that easily.
You say, "Why should we make speeches?
We already know how to talk."
I say, "'Yo, man' does not constitute
Effective communication between
    civilized beings."
You say, "I gotta go to the nurse."
I say, "Not unless you're bleeding internally."
You say, "Can't we just ad lib?"
I say, "Babbling is for babies."
I demand thought, preparation, and intelligence.
Talk may be cheap to some.
Not in my classroom, my darlings,
Not in my classroom.

Jocelyn Ridley
Period 7, Room 202

I think of all the adults in my life,
Adults with their pop-up questions.
"Why are you so quiet?"—my teacher.
("Well, I had this operation on
    my tongue and . . .")
"Why is your room so dirty?"—my mother.
("So the cockroaches can ride their dirt bikes.")
"Why aren't you planning for college?"
    —my father.
("I've been sold into white slavery
    —didn't I tell you?")
"Why don't you come to church?"—my priest.
("I've converted. I'm a Druid, I worship trees.")
Ms. Shaw, all these people
Keep hassling me with questions.
Can't you teach them how to listen instead?

Tammy Yarbrough
Period 7, Room 202

Last month when I gave my speech
My friend, Eileen, organized my notes,
Corrected my timing, applauded my delivery.
She even gave me a standing ovation.
Eileen sorta died last week.
I look at her empty chair,
Next to me in class,
And I feel like crying again.
Her parents took her away.
I couldn't bring myself to see her off
And now I feel horribly alone.
My friend, Eileen, didn't *really* die.
Her family just moved to a new city.
It's the same thing.
Please, Ms. Shaw,
I can't give my speech today.
There's nobody here to give me a hand.

Mercedes Lugo
Period 7, Room 202

Ms. Shaw,
If you want to know what's on my mind,
>Call me on the phone,
>Meet me in front of my house,
>Stop me on the corner,
>Pass me a note in the hall.
But don't ever, ever, ever
Expect me to stand up and
Give a speech that will
>Reveal my feelings,
>Tell the truth,
>Mean a whole lot,
>Make any sense.
I got nothing to say in class,
But a whole lot to say outside of it.

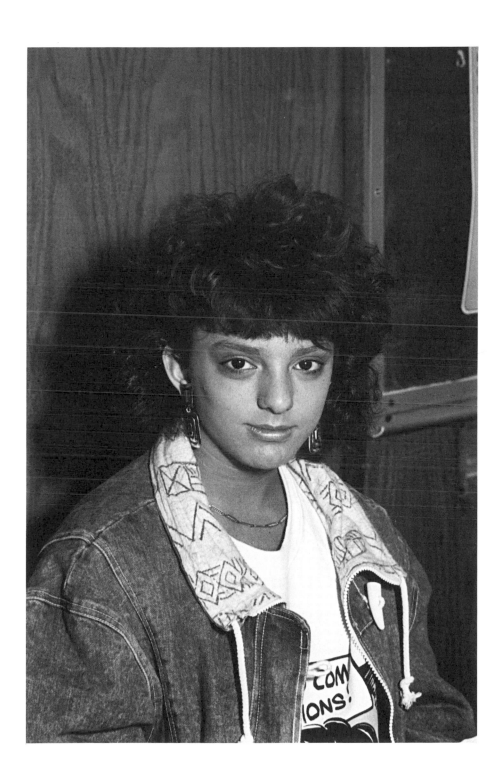

Hector Velasquez
Period 7, Room 202

Yeah, yeah, I know I was
Supposed to give my speech today.
But something came up.
Like this huge bump on my head.
Some creep beat up on my kid brother.
I got the guy,
This weirdo from my neighborhood.
I hit him good
And knocked out his two front teeth,
But not before he whacked me
On the back of the head with a stick.
I got the better of it,
I think.
You don't protect your own, you're nothin'.
Respect costs
And I got the scars that pay for it.
Yeah, my speech'll be ready tomorrow.
I'm speakin' about the constitutional right
To bear arms.

Ms. Joan Gladstone
Special Education
Period 8, Room 249

My special education children whirl around me
Like planets circling the sun.
I am the center of their universe.
Their faces reflect what light I give them,
Their chairs track close to my own.
If I shed too much light
On the dark side of their problems,
If I emit too much warmth
On the scarred terrain of their features,
I do more harm than good.
For I was not present
At the internal or external upheavals
That formed their pitted landscapes.
I cannot make up for
What was or wasn't there.
I do my job at a measured distance,
Skillfully, intelligently, professionally,
And when I go home to my own concerns
I make myself feel light years
Removed from their orbits.

Diana Marvin
Period 8, Room 249

Ms. Gladstone is real nice.
When I was having trouble with fractions
She came right over to help me.
I told her I get so confused with fractions.
I only understand part of it.
She said not to worry
And taught me how to change
Improper fractions into very proper ones.
She put her hand on my shoulder and said,
"Diana, you've really improved this year.
I'm so proud of you."
Ms. Gladstone is the best fractions teacher.
She takes pieces of what you know,
Of who you are,
And makes you feel whole.

Warren Christopher
Period 8, Room 249

My mother committed suicide when I was eight.
But I was crazy before that.
My psychiatrist says it has
Something to do with my older brother
Who banged his head against the wall.
I banged my head against the wall, too,
Because I didn't want him to feel alone.
My social worker says it has
Something to do with my father
Who would go out for cigarettes
And come back three weeks later,
Which was the length of time I'd cry.
My teacher says I have a bright future
If I do my work and pay attention.
She's a good teacher, but that don't
Change the fact that I'm in the dumb class.
I think I got scheduled for this class
A long, long time ago.

Bertha Robbins
Period 8, Room 249

I heard the preacher man ask,
"Is it not possible to be born again?"
What for?
So I can hear again
Names like "retard" and "moron"?
So I can try again
To learn to read right?
So I can fall again
For every sweet line
Guys use to lay me down?
I may be dumb,
But I ain't stupid.
I'm so smart I got a question that
I bet even the preacher man can't answer:
If God is supposed to love me,
Why did he make me like this?
Was it for something bad I done?

Frankie Dempster
Period 8, Room 249

When my brother
Was a teenager and I was not
He'd always tell me to stay in my room
When he brought his friends over.
And if I did come out
I shouldn't say or do anything stupid.
When my brother
Was in his twenties and I was fifteen
He'd always tell me to stay in my room
When he brought his girlfriends over.
And if I did come out
I shouldn't say or do anything stupid.
When my brother
Joined the army
He was in such a hurry to leave
That he didn't really say good-bye.
He just said, "See ya, kid."
I guess it's OK to come out of my room now.

C. C. Johnson
Period 8, Room 249

Ms. Gladstone, please tell me what to do.
I saw this boy at this club and
Our eyes met and well . . . you know,
One thing led to another,
Know what I mean?
He's the sweetest boyfriend I ever had.
He likes my eyes, my body,
My listening to him.
He has such plans and I—
I want to be part of his plans.
What's wrong?
Are you kidding?
I never told him I'm special ed.
What if he asks me to read or somethin'?
I'll die if he finds out.
Or should I tell him?
I know a lot of things,
But they don't have nothin' to do with school.
Please Ms. Gladstone, I don't want to lose him.
Tell me what to do.

Mr. Ted Sage
Accounting
Period 8, Room 219

Does it all add up?
I mean after all these years
Of roll books filled
And papers corrected,
Of some students passing
And others passing through,
Does it all add up
On the plus side of the ledger?
When all is said and done,
When my final class is dismissed,
As I close the doors on my professional career,
I would like to know with some assurance
What my net worth has been.
Have I meant something to someone?
A mind touched, a heart soothed,
A lesson learned and then applied?
Or have I been operating at a loss
In a system that is nearly
Educationally bankrupt?
Before my last entry is recorded
I'd like people to know
I tried my best,
So give me some credit.

Evan King
Period 8, Room 219

Mr. Sage tells very bad jokes,
Keeps us interested,
And encourages our best efforts.
Because of him I can balance a checkbook,
Compute profit and loss,
And handle a sales inventory.
In time I want my own business,
My own sports car,
And my own condo.
Right now in the afternoon
I deliver pizzas
And in summer I sell door to door.
My father, who drives a bus,
Asks me what the rush is,
Says I'll be working full time soon enough,
Right now I should relax, he says,
Explore the world,
Read great works of literature,
And find out who I am.
My father, who means well, doesn't realize
That growing up requires tough
        business decisions,
Thanks to Mr. Sage's accounting class
I'm getting a jump on
My competition.

Abby Kramer
Period 8, Room 219

Every time my father gets angry with me
For something I've done or haven't done
I just smile at him and he says, "Never mind."
I have him totally snowed.
Every time my boyfriend wants me to go
Someplace I wouldn't be caught dead at
I just smile at him and he says, "Never mind."
I have him totally confused.
Every time my boss wants me to work late
And there is something else I'd rather do
I just smile at him and he says, "Never mind."
I have him totally charmed.
It's not all that difficult to understand males.
Remember two things:
That, emotionally, they are all twelve years old,
And that cute and adorable
Beats plain and responsible
Every time.

Charlene Cottier
Period 8, Room 219

My father still calls me his little girl.
I'm seventeen years old,
Look like a woman,
Especially when I'm dressed up,
And he still thinks I'm seven.
He insists on driving me to school,
Wants to know who all my friends are,
And you should only know
The battle I went through
To get his permission to go out on dates.
Once, when a brave young man
Came to pick me up
My father started grilling the guy,
Asking him what his intentions were.
I could have died right then and there.
Daddy, please let me go.
Grown women can love their fathers too,
    you know.

Elliot West
Period 8, Room 219

Mr. Sage is very fond of saying:
    "Where will you fall out
    On the ledger of life?"
We groan; he continues merrily:
    "Will you be a credit
    Or a liability to yourself?"
We groan louder; he ignores us:
    "You are an unknown risk.
    Will people profit from knowing you?"
We whistle; he shouts over us:
    "Your life is a clean record book.
    Make your own entries upon it."
We boo; he has one more thing to say:
    "I teach you numbers, but
    Figure out your own way.
    Use your assets,
    Trust your judgement.
    You'll come out all right,
        On balance."

About the Author

Mel Glenn was born in Switzerland, grew up in Brooklyn, New York, and served in the Peace Corps in West Africa in the 1960s. Today, he teaches at the school where he was once a student, Abraham Lincoln High School in Brooklyn. He and his wife, Elyse, who is also a teacher, have two sons, Jonathan and Andrew. Mr. Glenn has written two novels, *One Order to Go* and *Play-by-Play*, as well as two other books of high school poems, *Class Dismissed!* and *Class Dismissed II*.

About the Photographer

Michael J. Bernstein is an assistant principal for science at Lafayette High School in Brooklyn, where many of these photographs were taken. He and his wife, Joanne, who is a writer, live in Brooklyn with their two children, Robin and Andrew. Mr. Bernstein took the photographs for *Dmitry: A Young Soviet Immigrant* written by his wife. He also provided the photographs for *Class Dismissed!* and *Class Dismissed II*.